/14

Howard B. Wigglebottom

On Yes or No

A Fable About Trust

Howard Binkow Reverend Ana

Taillefer Long

Howard B. Wigglebottom was a very curious bunny.

He needed to know how every little thing worked.

"Why did you say this?"

"Why did you do that?"

"How is this made? Why is it like that?"

He often asked.

So when his friend Buzz was unhappy and getting in trouble all the time

Howard had to find out why.

On the first day Howard saw Kiki asking Buzz
for a bite of his pizza.

"Look up.

There goes a superhero."

Then—as usual—she tricked him and ran away with the whole slice.

On the second day Howard saw Poochie skating away with Buzz's games. "Poochie loses or breaks what he borrows," cried Buzz..

8

On the third day Howard saw Buzz getting into big trouble. Oinky—who was grounded most of the time—talked Buzz into stealing a cupcake.

Stealing is so wrong! thought Howard. How could Buzz go for that?

On the fourth day Howard saw Buzz's stuff all over the steps.

He was crying again: "They said on TV my backpack would never break. Mom was right; they lie on TV commercials sometimes."

On the fifth day Howard saw Buzz accepting a ride from a stranger!
So Howard screamed, "NOOOO!" and the stranger drove away.
"Buzz," Howard said, "we all know not to speak to strangers when grownups
are not around. Why would you do that?"

Buzz explained he had a hard time saying NO.
He wanted everyone to like him.
He didn't know when not to believe or trust people.

16

"Aha" said Howard.
"Now I know what is wrong!
Let's ask the grownups for some ideas."

Buzz needed to know when to say No
and when to say Yes.

19

After asking many people, they learned:
Buzz was to say NO, and not speak to
or trust any stranger until a teacher or a
grownup from his family said OK.

"Even if the stranger is nice and wants to give me nice things?" asked Buzz. "Yes!" said Howard. "You must run away. Always run away."

"Say NO to anyone who has wronged and hurt you before.
Don't trust them!" said Howard.
"Oh!" said Buzz, getting sad. "What if they think I'm not nice?"

Howard pointed out to Buzz that everyone likes superheroes, artists and athletes who stand up and say No when they need to.

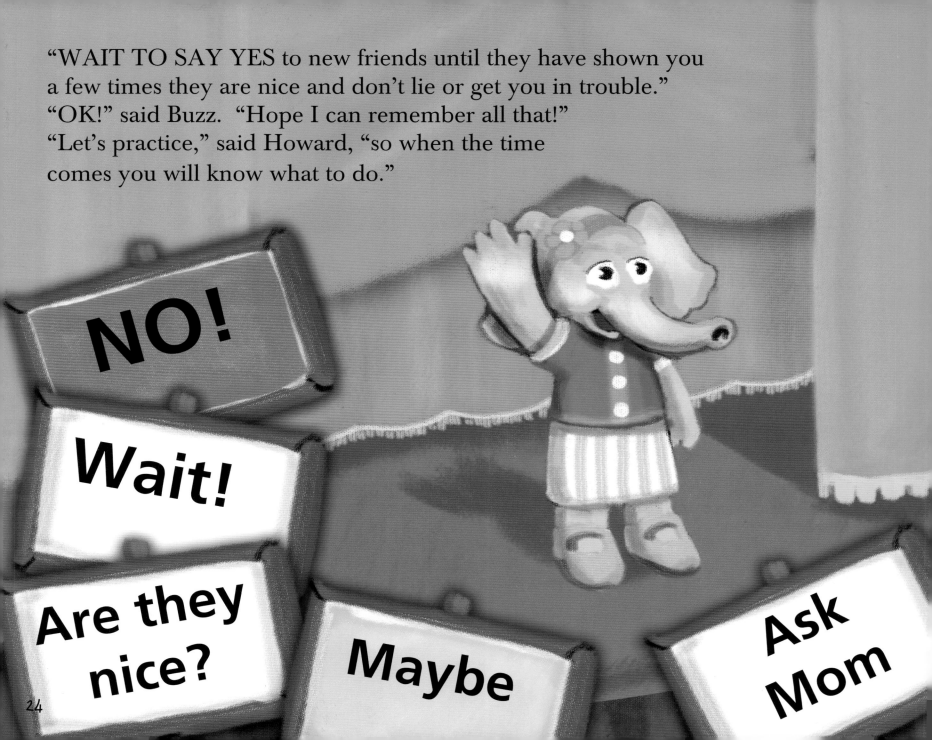

"WAIT TO SAY YES to new friends until they have shown you a few times they are nice and don't lie or get you in trouble."
"OK!" said Buzz. "Hope I can remember all that!"
"Let's practice," said Howard, "so when the time comes you will know what to do."

NO!

Wait!

Are they nice?

Maybe

Ask Mom

For the next few days Howard watched Buzz saying NO to bad friends and a strong NO! to a grownup stranger.

They kept watch to see who could be trusted, so they would know who they could make friends with and say Yes to.

Howard was very proud of Buzz.
He had learned WHEN to say
Yes and No, to defend himself
and to be happy again!

Off they went to play and have fun...

Howard B. Wigglebottom Learns about Trust and Friends

Suggestions for Lessons and Reflections

Good friends tell the truth, are nice, will ask permission to take our toys or food and never get us in trouble.

We can always trust good friends.

Do you know what trust means?

To trust or to believe—same thing—is to feel sure about something, to think it's true. Can we trust or believe everything and everybody? Not really. If we want to be safe and happy it is best to follow the rules about trust.

★ TRUST RULE #1: We can only believe or trust our friends when they always tell the truth, keep their promises, and are nice to us.

If they cheat, lie, tell our secrets, don't keep promises, never help out, steal, hurt us, or make us do things we don't care to, they cannot be trusted. We can't believe anything they say.

Did Buzz trust Howard? Yes, Buzz trusted Howard because Howard was a good friend.

Whom can you trust in your house and at school? Do your friends trust you?

Did Buzz have bad friends? Yes. Kiki, Oinky and Poochie weren't nice; they cheated, lied, broke things, and got him in trouble. Did Buzz trust the bad friends? Only in the beginning. Once he learned the rules he stopped trusting the bad friends.

What is the difference between a good friend and a bad one?

Do you have good friends?

What about bad ones?

Are you a good friend to your friends?

What happens when old friends change?

★ TRUST RULE #2: If old friends start lying or hurting us we stop trusting them—we don't believe what they say anymore. If they want us to trust them again they will have to repeat being nice and truthful many, many times.

Can we trust new kids we just met?

★ TRUST RULE #3: When we meet new people it is hard to tell if they are going to be nice and tell the truth or not. Grownups have a saying, "trust is earned," that means before we give new friends our trust we need to wait and see if they are nice for sure.

Play with the new kid several days and pay attention: is the new kid nice to us and our things every time? Many, many days in a row? Does the new kid tell the truth?

If the answer is yes, then we can trust and believe the new friend!

The same rule applies to the things you hear on TV commercials, shows, movies, and games. Before you believe—trust what you hear—ask a grownup to help you find out if it is true or not.

Learning when to trust and believe, when to say yes or no, is a very important thing to keep us safe and happy.

★ IT'S SUPER OK TO SAY NO

It is not easy to say no to friends or to people we look up to. Just like eating and brushing our teeth, learning to say no is something we all need to do.

When we are very young we think if we say no when we need to people will not like us anymore. That is not true. Like Howard told Buzz on page 23, people who say no when they need to are cool and strong. We all look up to strong people!

When did Buzz need to say no? He needed to say no to Kiki because she was cheating him, to Poochie because he was not careful with borrowed toys, to Oinky because he wanted to steal.

We must always say no to friends we can't trust or believe anything they say, even if they tell us they don't like us anymore.

It is always OK to say no to good friends, whenever we need to. Do it nicely, say thank you, smile, and explain why. Stand your ground!!

Saying no when we need to is the first step of learning how to protect and defend ourselves. Saying no makes us strong!

When do you need to say NO to good friends? If they want to share some food you don't like or you are not supposed to eat, if they want to do something in your house your parents or guardians don't like, if they want you to disobey rules, and if they are not careful with your things.

Can you think of more examples when you need to say no to good friends? What do you do when your good friends say no to you?

★ STRANGER DANGER

We never speak to strangers and never, but never accept anything strangers want to give us unless a grownup we know says it's OK. Why is that? Because we can't tell if strange people are nice or not, if they want to hurt us and take us away or not. So if a stranger is trying to talk to you, RUN! Run away as fast as you can, even if the stranger says things like "come help me find my puppy," "come here; I have cool things to give to you," or "come inside my ice cream truck."

We always say no to strangers even if they say we are not nice and they don't like us!

Saying no to strangers make us super strong and powerful!

Learn more about Howard's other adventures.

BOOKS

Howard B. Wigglebottom Learns to Listen

Howard B. Wigglebottom Listens to His Heart

Howard B. Wigglebottom Learns About Bullies

Howard B. Wigglebottom Learns About Mud and Rainbows

Howard B. Wigglebottom Learns It's OK to Back Away

Howard B. Wigglebottom and the Monkey on His Back:
A Tale About Telling the Truth

Howard B. Wigglebottom Learns Too Much of a Good Thing Is Bad

Howard B. Wigglebottom and the Power of Giving: A Christmas Story

Howard B. Wigglebottom Blends in Like Chameleons:
A Fable About Belonging

Howard B. Wigglebottom Learns About Sportsmanship:
Winning isn't Everything

Howard B. Wigglebottom Learns About Courage

WEBSITE
Visit www.wedolisten.org

• Enjoy free animated books, games, and songs.

• Print lessons and posters from the books.

• Email the author.

31

Howard Binkow
Reverend Ana
Illustration by Taillefer Long
Book design by Jane Darroch Riley

Thunderbolt Publishing
We Do Listen Foundation
www.wedolisten.org

Gratitude and appreciation are given to all those who reviewed the story prior to publication;
the book became much better by incorporating several of their suggestions:

Karen Binkow, Darlene Demell, Joanne De Graaf, Amanda Dunville, Leigh Fox, Trish Jones, Lisa Kascak, Laurie and Charlie Kowalski,
Kathy Rule, Julia Simpson, Laurie Sachs, George Sachs-Walor, Nancey Silvers, Erinn Sluka, Rosemary Underwood,
and the teachers, counselors, media specialists and children at:

Cummings Elementary School, Misawa Air Base, Japan
Garden Elementary, Venice, Florida
Lamarque Elementary, Northport, Florida
Sherman Oaks Elementary, Sherman Oaks, California

First printing March 2013
Printed in Malaysia by Tien Wah Press (Pte) Limited.

ISBN 978-0-9826165-8-1

LCCN 2013933130